THE TIME WARP TRIO series

THE TIME WARP TRIO

Hey Kid, Want to Buy a Bridge?

by Jon Scieszka

illustrated by Adam McCauley

SCHOLASTIC INC.

New York Toronto London Auckland Sydney
Mexico City New Delhi Hong Kong Buenos Aires

ISBN 0-439-53110-1

Text copyright © 2002 by Jon Scieszka.
Illustrations copyright © 2002 by Adam McCauley.
All rights reserved.
Published by Scholastic Inc., 557 Broadway, New York, NY 10012,
by arrangement with Viking Children's Books,
a member of Penguin Putnam Inc. SCHOLASTIC and associated logos
are trademarks and/or registered trademarks of Scholastic Inc.

12 11 10 9 8 7 6 5 4 3 2 1   3 4 5 6 7 8/0

Printed in the U.S.A.   40

First Scholastic printing, September 2003

Set in Sabon

ONE

"Whoa," said Fred. "The Brooklyn Bridge is missing a few pieces."

"No skyscrapers anywhere," said Sam, fixing his glasses and looking all around us.

I stood there with my trick rope hanging from my wrist. "Somebody took the Statue of Liberty," I said, looking out into the New York harbor.

Sam stamped both feet. "I told you something like this would happen. How come no one ever listens to me? This does not look good."

I looked around and realized Sam was absolutely right.

In the early morning light I could see that the three of us were standing on top of one of the towers of the Brooklyn Bridge. The other tower was across the river. Wind whistled through our legs. Two seagulls flew around our heads. We were the tallest thing for miles around.

But that wasn't
the not-good part.
The not-good part
was what wasn't there.
The whole bridge and
wires and almost all of
the stuff between the towers wasn't there. The Empire
State Building, the Chrysler
Building, every skyscraper wasn't
there. The thin blue book with silver
designs that used to be on the other
end of the rope tied to my wrist . . .
wasn't anywhere.

The only thing left of the Brooklyn
Bridge was the two towers, a couple of
wires, and one very skinny footbridge that
went from the ground to our tower, across
the river to the other tower, and back down to
the ground in Brooklyn on the other side.

"Just like I said would happen. We've gone
too far in the future," said Sam. "All of New York
has been taken over by mutant space aliens. Your
plan to meet up with our great-granddaughters
didn't work. And your foolproof invention to

hold on to *The Book* got fooled." Sam paced around in a mad little circle. "And once again . . . we will never get back home!" he screamed into the wind.

Fred pushed his Brooklyn Cyclones hat back on his head and looked down over the edge.

"That's weird," he said. "Do mutant space aliens use sailboats?"

Sam and I looked down. We saw a whole line of those giant sailboats with three masts that you see in old pictures and on sailors' tattoos in cartoons. It sure didn't look like the future we visited last time, in 2095.

"Oh no," said Sam, pulling his hair with both hands. "This is even worse."

"What?" I said. "What's so bad about sailboats?"

"That would explain everything," said Sam.

Fred and I looked at each other. We had no idea what Sam was talking about. But we know Sam by now. We know if you just let him rant long enough, he'll eventually get to the point.

"No skyscrapers. No Statue of Liberty. No Brooklyn Bridge," ranted Sam. "No motorboats, no cars, no jets. We didn't go too far in the future. We went into the past. No one has invented sky-scrapers yet. They haven't finished building the Brooklyn Bridge!"

"But how did *The Book* backfire us into the past? And why are we on the top of this bridge tower?" I said. "We were talking about the future, and inventions, and our great-granddaughters."

"Yeah," said Fred. "What the—*ahhhhh!*" Fred pointed behind us.

A dark shadowy figure was crawling up onto the tower from the shorter footbridge leading to the ground behind us. It looked up at us through beady eyes stuck in a mess of wild hair. When it saw us, it lifted a long club and roared.

"Mutant space alien!" yelled Sam, forgetting his theory about us going into the past.

Fred grabbed a baseball-sized stone, wound up, and pitched a perfect beanball. The stone bounced off the mutant guy's noggin. He dropped down on one knee, but then got up looking madder than ever. He swung his club and roared something again.

We looked at the wild hairy thing on the Manhattan side in front of us. We looked at the long skinny footbridge swinging over the water to Brooklyn behind us. And we took exactly one second to decide which way to go.

"Brooklyn!" yelled Fred, running for the other tower.

"Brooklyn!" I yelled, following Fred over the swaying footpath.

"Oh man," said Sam, holding both hand-wires, trying to not look down at the river swirling far below us, and running for his life.

TWO

But before we take our chances—running across a bridge about as wide as a baseball bat is long, swinging in the wind higher above a river than I've ever been—I'd like to put in a good word for Fred and Sam and myself.

I know in the past we have maybe not been too swift about using *The Book*. It's a very tricky thing, this book. You would think anyone would know how to work a book. But if you were thinking that about *this* book . . . you'd be wrong.

I got *The Book* for my birthday from my Uncle Joe, the magician. Well, he tries to be a magician. To tell you the truth, he's awful. But he has taught me a few good tricks. And this book he gave me turns out to be real magic. It's thin, dark blue with strange silver writing and designs on it. And one more thing—the best trick of all—this book can somehow transport Fred and Sam and me anywhere in time.

We have climbed pyramids in ancient Egypt, fought gladiators in Rome, met our own great-granddaughters one hundred years in the future, and got into a whole mess of other history in between.

That's the good news.

The bad news is that the only way to get back home to our time is to find *The Book* in the time we travel to. And so far, no matter what we have tried, we cannot seem to hold on to *The Book*.

We've also had a little trouble—okay, Sam would probably tell you anyway—a lot of trouble figuring out how and where *The Book* takes us. We usually just get whipped off someplace in time by the green mist that leaks out of *The Book* when we look at a picture, or say a haiku, or who knows what. . . .

But not this time.

This time we had a plan. This time we knew where we wanted to go. This time we'd planned how we were going to hang on to *The Book*. This time we were going to be successful time warpers.

Or so we thought.

Fred, Sam, and I were down in the basement of my house in our neighborhood in Brooklyn. Sam was looking for a cable to "input the Graphi-Tronic Bing Bong" into his Game Boy. Or something like that. Fred was seeing how many times he could bounce his Wiffle ball off Sam's head before Sam freaked out. I was working on my latest rope trick.

That's where things started to go wrong.

"So what is this Grapho-Monic thing supposed to do?" I asked.

Sam dug through one of my dad's boxes of electrical junk. My dad's got a million boxes of strange stuff for anything you could imagine from all of his travels around the world.

Sam fiddled with a plug to connect a mini-microphone he had taken from an old computer to a box he had made from his Game Boy. "My invention is called a Graphi-Sonic. I'm turning the sound waves of my voice into digital images on the screen of my Game Boy."

Fred curled the brim of his new Brooklyn Cyclones hat and bounced another Wiffle-ball toss off Sam's head. "What for?"

"I'm inventing," said Sam. "Like Thomas

Edison. Did you know he had more than one thousand inventions? My Graphi-Sonic could turn out to be the next telephone or lightbulb or something." Sam plugged in his Graphi-Sonic.

Fred bounced another beanball off Sam's head.

"Cut it out, Fred," said Sam. "Watch the screen." He spoke into the microphone. "Mary had a little lamb."

We looked at the screen. Nothing.

Sam fiddled with a few connections and tried again. "Mary had a little lamb."

We looked at the screen. Nothing.

"Gaahhh!" Sam groaned. "I give up. What's the use? How am I supposed to invent anything? All of the good inventions have already been invented."

Fred bounced another toss off Sam's head. "Yeah, like the Wiffle ball. Did you know it was invented by a guy in Connecticut in 1952? His name was David Mullany. He made it for his kid to throw curve balls without messing up his arm or breaking windows. He took a bunch of plastic balls and cut holes in them to find the best pattern to make curves. And this was it." Fred held up his Wiffle ball.

I was stunned. I've never heard Fred say that many words in a row . . . ever.

Sam sat with his head down, looking at his Graphi-Sonic in his lap. He looked completely crushed. Not even Fred's speech or the ball bouncing off his head got through to him. We had to do something to help his invention.

I thought for a second. And that's when I came up with the plan.

"I've got it," I said.

I crawled under the old wooden workbench and reached up to a hidden shelf. I pulled out a thin blue book covered with strange silver designs and writing. I pulled out *The Book*.

Sam didn't even twitch. That's when I knew something was really wrong with him. Usually just the sight of *The Book* is enough to send him running.

I held *The Book* in my lap. "What if we went into the future, like when we first met our great-granddaughters? You could find a great invention, figure out how it works, and then come back here to invent it in this time."

Sam didn't look up. "It probably wouldn't work. We'd probably go too far into the future. All of New York would be taken over by mutant space aliens."

Fred stopped bouncing his Wiffle ball off Sam's noggin. Now even Fred could see this was serious. "We could just go as far as we went last time. We'd stay right here in Brooklyn, check out our great-granddaughters' future stuff, and come right back. How much trouble could we get into in our own neighborhood?"

"And look at this," I said. "I've invented a fool-proof Book Tracker." I took my thick rope, knotted one end around *The Book*, then knotted the other end around my wrist.

Sam didn't even crack a smile. "I give up."

Fred and I looked at each other. This was serious.

"Come on, you weenie," said Fred.

"So what—" I started to say.

And that's when Sam's Graphi-Sonic invention

beeped. The screen flashed a pattern of green lines. *The Book* flashed back and leaked a puff of green mist.

We didn't know what we did, but we did know we did it.

The green mist popped and exploded all around us in a mini-cyclone. Without knowing how, why, or where—we were time-warp gone.

THREE

We ran like crazy guys out over the river between Manhattan and Brooklyn on the littlest bridge you can imagine. It's amazing what being afraid will make you do. We ran almost halfway across before we even looked back.

The thing was still standing back on the tower, waving its club. It was still yelling at us.

"What was that?" said Fred.

"I don't know," I said. "But it must be afraid to come out over the river and smash to death below."

"Ooooh," groaned Sam. He grabbed the hand wires. "Thanks for reminding me of that wonderful possibility."

The footbridge swung sideways and wiggled up and down all at once.

"Let's go," I said.

"I can't," said Sam.

"Can't what?" I said.

"Can't . . . move. . . ." said Sam. He squeezed the wires even harder and closed his eyes. I guess the fear of the mutant thing had worn off. Now complete fear of the bridge was sinking in.

"Come on," said Fred. "We're not going to let some hairy mutant have us for breakfast. Let's get over to that tower and back home to Brooklyn."

"Urrrgh," said Sam.

Fred jumped into action. You can always count on him to do something when the going gets tough. He got me behind Sam on the bridge. He peeled one of Sam's hands off the wire and put it on his own shoulder. Then we started moving. All together. Step by step. Very slowly. Sam barely peeking out of one eye. But we were moving. And the thing wasn't following us . . . yet.

We inched up to the Brooklyn tower, stepped onto the top, and just about fell right off. Because there on the top of the tower, sitting in a circle, talking to an intense-looking young guy in a suit, were our three great-granddaughters—Joanie,

Samantha, and Frieda (or J, Samza, and Freddi as they prefer to be called).

Fred and I stood there with our mouths hanging open. Sam dropped down to feel the solid stone.

The girls looked over at us. They didn't look really happy to see us.

"I told you they were behind this," said Samza. "Why doesn't anyone ever listen to me?"

"Uh, hi girls," I said. "What's up?"

"What's up?" said Samza. "More like, what's messed up? More like, how did you ever manage to get things so messed up?"

"Boy, we sure are glad to see you, too," said Fred.

Freddi waved to us. She was wearing a baseball hat that looked like Fred's Cyclones hat. We walked over and sat down. It's always weird when we first see our great-granddaughters from one hundred years in our future. We never know what to say to them.

"Hi guys," said J. "Samza is always a little loco after she time warps. But she gets really fa kuang when she doesn't know where or why she's warping."

"We've figured out that we're definitely back a few years before the Brooklyn Bridge is finished," said Freddi, writing on a small green pad.

"1877," said Samza, pushing one side of her black glasses. "The towers were finished by 1876. All the cable was done by 1878. So we are somewhere between those two dates."

"Right," said Sam, turning back to almost a normal color now that he had some facts to work with.

"But what about the mutant space aliens that took over New York and chased us off the other tower?" I said. The girls looked at me like they had just stepped on a giant dog dropping.

"Que—what?" all three said together.

"That mutant on the tower over there waving his club at us," I said.

"Him?" said Freddi. "He's probably just a bridge guard. They do let people walk across, but it's too early in the morning. So he chased you off. Where did you ever get the idea he was a mutant space alien?"

I looked at Sam.

Sam was suddenly very interested in looking at his shoe.

"But more importantly," said Samza, frowning at me with her glowing blue-black eyes, "What in the world did you do to *The Book* to bring us here? And what did you do to drag Alva into this?"

"Who's Alva?" asked Fred.

J pointed to the guy in the suit. He sat on one of the wires, looking completely dazed.

"I give up," said the man.

Sam's eyes bugged out of his head.

"Alva?" said Sam. I knew Sam had just figured out something that wasn't good.

Samza nodded.

"Thomas Alva?" asked Sam.

Samza nodded.

"Come on, you weenie," said the man.

Now it was Fred's turn to bug his eyes out.

"Oh no," said Sam.

"Oh yes," said Samza.

"Would someone please tell me what's with this guy named Thomas Alva?" said Fred.

"That's Thomas Alva," said Sam. "As in Thomas Alva Edison, inventor of the phonograph and the lightbulb and a thousand other things that changed the world."

"Oh, that Thomas Alva," said Fred.

"So what," said Thomas Alva Edison.

"He just keeps saying those same three things over and over," said J.

Samza adjusted her glasses again. "You guys have really done it this time. *The Book* doesn't usually affect anyone else. But whatever you did to it dragged us here, and wrecked Thomas Edison." Samza was getting worked up now. "This is the man who was probably the hardest working inventor ever. This is the man who said inventing is one percent inspiration and ninety-nine percent perspiration. And you've got him saying 'I give up' and 'So what' and—and—and—"

Samza was so mad she couldn't say anything else.

The wind whipped around us. Down below on

18

the Brooklyn side I could see carts pulled by horses beginning to move around the city streets. Sailboats began gliding out of the harbor. Steamboat ferries churned back and forth. And now there was a good chance that things might stay just like this for a very long time if we didn't untangle this mess. Who knows what other inventions might not happen? This was definitely not good.

"I give up," said Edison.

"Don't say that, T.," said Fred. "No lightbulbs, no music, no movies? Guys, we have got to do something."

"Rapido," agreed Freddi.

I agreed. But then I thought about it, and realized—I didn't have the foggiest idea what that something might be.

FOUR

We all sat on top of the unfinished Brooklyn Bridge tower. Three guys from more than one hundred years in the future. Three girls from more than two hundred years in the future. One guy from the present. All of us in danger of having no future.

J was the first to speak. Sitting cross-legged, she flipped back her long blonde hair. "The most obvious thing we have to do is find *The Book*."

"Even then," said Samza, "we might not be able to re-warp over this whole mess and fix it." She tried to flip her dark purple hair back like J did, but only ended up making it stick out in all directions. "Especially if you Sonic Warped us all here."

Sam and I looked at each other. I guess it was a guilty look.

"You didn't use the Sonic Warp, did you?" said Samza. "Tell me you didn't Sonic Warp."

"Well," I said, knotting and unknotting my rope, "Sam was working on his invention. . . ."

"But I call my invention the Graphi-Sonic," said Sam.

"And we were talking about going into the future to check out your time and maybe bring back a few invention ideas—" I started to explain.

Samza turned to J. "They did Sonic Warp. That's where you activate *The Book* by a voice pattern. *The Book* translates the sounds into instructions."

"Hey," said Sam. "That's almost like the invention I was working on."

"Well, thanks for wrecking Thomas Edison and civilization and dragging us into it too," said Samza.

"You're welcome," said Sam. "Thanks for being so helpful yourself."

Fred couldn't take any more. He held up both hands. "Hold it. Hold it. Hooold it. What the heck are you talking about? We didn't do anything. We were just talking about stuff."

"Exactamente," said Samza. "You triggered

21

The Book with voice commands. You dragged me, J, and Freddi back here. You knocked the will to invent right out of Thomas Alva Edison. And you lost *The Book*. Any more questions?"

"So what," said Edison.

Fred pulled down his hat. "Well we're not going to get anything fixed by talking about it. Let's get down from here, find *The Book*, and get Thomas Alva Edison back to inventing. Come on, T." Fred

helped Edison to his feet and headed for the narrow footbridge down to the ground.

"Oh," said Freddi. Then she turned that same ghost white Sam had been a few minutes earlier.

"Don't tell me you're afraid of bridges, too," said Fred.

"I'm not afraid," said Freddi, not moving off the solid stones. "It's just that I think we should . . . um . . . well . . . sit down and talk about this a bit longer."

"You are chicken," said Fred. "I'm going." He turned to grab Edison's arm, and then suddenly yelled, "*Ahhhhh!*"

We looked behind us and saw what had made him yell. There on the edge of the foot- bridge from the other tower stood—the mutant space alien with the club.

"*Ahhhhhh!*" we all yelled and jumped to our feet.

The mutant guy jumped down and rapped his club on the stone.

"Stop yer wild yellin'," it said.

We stopped and looked closer. The guy wasn't a space alien. He was only a not-very-friendly-looking guy with an ugly mess of beard and whiskers. The smooth round black hat jammed on his head and his ugly mug just made him look like a mutant. The club in his hand was an old-fashioned baseball bat.

"We've had enough of yer vandal types messing with good men's work up here." Ugly Mug knocked his bat on the stone again and used it to point to the footpath. "Down! Right now! Every one of yer. I'll teach yer rascals a thing or two."

"Come on, you weenie," said Edison to no one in particular.

"What was that?" said Ugly Mug.

Freddi put a hand over Edison's mouth. "He said it's very scenic."

"Urrrgh," said Ugly Mug. "Get moving."

We were all so freaked out we didn't argue. Even Sam and Freddi were more afraid of the guy with the bat than they were of small bridges way off the ground. We shuffled in a

24

line down the footbridge to the cable anchoring platform.

I looked out over the strangely low buildings and old-fashioned gas lamps and sailboats on the water. I quit worrying about what might happen to a world without electricity and lightbulbs and phonographs. I started worrying about what exactly Ugly Mug was planning on teaching us.

FIVE

The walk down the footpath to the anchor tower wasn't quite as scary as the walk across the river. It was kind of amazing to look over the top of all of Brooklyn from a long time ago. No cars, no buses, no subways. The smell of chimney smoke and horses and the ocean in the air.

Sam and Freddi weren't too excited about the sightseeing. By the time we reached the bottom, they both looked like they were going to lose their lunch.

"Oh," said Freddi.

"Oh," moaned Sam.

"I give up," said Edison.

"T, put a sock in it, would you?" said Fred.

We stepped off the footbridge onto another stone platform—this one about as high as a four- or five-story building.

"This way," said Ugly Mug. He marched us all

into a wooden shed half filled with spools of wire and huge metal bars.

We stuck together close to one wall. Ugly Mug faced us, holding his bat in one meaty hand, and smacking it into his other meaty mitt.

I think we all suddenly realized what might be worse than not having lightbulbs or phonographs in the future. It might just be worse to get knocked with a bat in the present.

I didn't know what to do. So I pulled out my piece of rope.

Ugly Mug looked confused. But at least he quit smacking his bat. I decided it would be good to keep him interested.

"Ugly Mu—I mean Mr. Guard Mug," I said. "We are very sorry we ended up on your bridge and thought you were a mutant space—"

"A what?" growled Ugly Mug.

"A nothing," I said. "Forget it. I mean we are not vandals."

J stepped up next to me. "No, not at all. We are an official group."

Ugly Mug scratched his neck. "What kinder group?"

"So what," said Edison.

"Whadid yer say to me?" said Ugly Mug.

Samza sat Edison down on a wooden box and said, "A magic group."

"Yeah, that's it," I said. "We're a magic group and this is a magic rope that can knot and unknot itself and we were . . . uh . . ."

". . . studying the knots on the bridge," added Freddi.

Now Ugly Mug looked very confused. "What are yer talkin about?"

I realized I had no idea what I was talking about. I was just talking to keep from getting smacked with that bat.

"So . . . observe!" I held the length of rope up with a dramatic arm move. "I can form knots or make them disappear any time I want."

"Oh really?" said Ugly Mug.

I suddenly wished I had practiced this trick a few more times.

I looped the rope into a big U. But then I couldn't remember which way to put the loop to form the sliding knot.

"You just put it like this . . ."

(I guessed.)

"Pull the rope . . ."

(This is the place where the knot was supposed to fall apart.)

"...and...it is..."

(I pulled. The knot stuck.)

"...a knot!"

Ugly Mug looked annoyed now. "Dat's stupid. Put the rope down."

"But now ..." J said, grabbing the rope.

"I hold the rope the same way." She did.

"I knot it the same way." She did.

"Pull the rope and—the knot disappears!" And it did.

Ugly Mug smiled. I started to breathe again.

"Remind me to show that trick to your grandmother," I said to J.

"Exactly where I learned it," said J.

"Dat's real nice," said Ugly Mug. "Now I'm gonna

show yer my trick." And without any more warn-ing, he lifted his bat over one shoulder and stepped toward us.

Fred grabbed a metal bar, but it was too heavy to lift. The rest of us, except Edison, dove behind the boxes and wires.

"Come on, you weenie," said Edison.

At that very second, the sunlight dimmed. Someone was standing in the doorway.

"Mr. Mug," said the someone. "What is going on here?"

Mr. Mug squinted toward the figure. I couldn't believe it. The guy's last name really was "Mug." I wondered if his first name really was "Ugly."

"Mis-Mis-Mister Roebling? I-I-I caught these vandals on yer bridge and I was, well, yer know . . ."

"These are hardly vandals, Mr. Mug. You may go."

Mr. Mug disappeared even more suddenly than he had appeared.

"Mr. Roebling?" said Samza.

"Yes?" answered the bearded man in the suit and hat.

"Mr. Roebling who designed and built the Brooklyn Bridge?"

"Well, I'm trying my best to get this bridge built. I haven't been down here to the site since the towers went up. But this morning I felt . . . I don't know." He took off his hat and sat down next to Edison.

"I give up," said Edison.

"So what," said Mr. Roebling.

"Ay yi," said Freddi. "I think it's catching."

"We have got to get *The Book* NOW," said Samza. "Otherwise this is going to keep spreading. And there will be no lightbulbs, no Brooklyn Bridge, no future, no us."

SIX

"**I** give up," said Washington Roebling, Chief Engineer of the Brooklyn Bridge.

"So what," said Thomas Alva Edison, inventor of the lightbulb and the phonograph.

"We have one big problem," said Samza, great-granddaughter of Sam.

"Well if you're such a time travel expert, why don't you tell us how to fix this?" said Sam.

"If you're such a genius, tell me the voice command you used on *The Book*," said Samza. "Then maybe we can undo this."

"I have no idea," said Sam.

"You said it," said Samza.

"I don't know," said Sam.

"You should," said Samza.

"I don't."

"Well try."

"Get lost!"

"We're going to be!"

"Washington!" said a woman's voice. The owner of the voice, a dark-haired lady in a long blue dress, swept into the shack, just in time to stop Sam and Samza from strangling each other. She hurried over to Mr. Roebling.

"Washington, are you well? I looked everywhere for you. One of the men told me you were up here."

Washington Roebling gave a small nod. "I give up," he said.

"So what," said Edison.

"What?" said the lady.

I figured I'd better start talking before Roebling and Edison said any more to get us in trouble.

"Mr. Roebling came to, uh, help us," I said. "Because we are visitors from . . . uh . . .visitors from."

"Mexico," said Freddi.

"And China," said J.

The lady looked us over. I don't know what she thought of us—three guys in jeans and T-shirts from one hundred years in the future and three girls in strange clothes from two hundred years in the future.

"Uh-hum," said the lady.

"We are so busted now," Fred whispered to me. "What were those girls thinking?"

"My name is Emily Roebling," said the lady. "My husband has not been completely well since the construction of the towers. In fact, he's never been down here since. He usually watches the work from our house." She pointed down the Brooklyn waterfront. "But you must be special visitors for him to meet you here."

"Oh yes," said Sam. "Very special."

"Gracias," said Freddi. "Gracias por your favor."

"Xie xie," said J.

Mrs. Roebling gave a little bow. The girls speaking Spanish and Chinese got her to believe us . . . for now. I thought we'd better get out while the getting was good, before she asked any more questions.

"Well thank you and good-bye," I said.

"Adios," said Samza.

"Zai jian," said J.

"We're off to the . . . um . . . uh . . . erh . . ." I couldn't think where we might be off to.

"The library," said Freddi.

"Right—the library," I said, pushing everyone out the door.

Freddi grabbed Edison's hand so he would come with us.

"Thank you, Mrs. Roebling. And don't worry about Mr. Roebling," I said. "Everything will be okay once we find our *Book*."

We all piled out the door of the shack. Mrs. Roebling held Mr. Roebling's hand and gave us one last funny look. We found some stairs on the side of the tower and zigzagged our way down at least ten flights of wooden steps.

"That was a good trick," I said to J. "How do you know Spanish and Chinese?"

"Everybody in New York does," said J. "Oh, I forgot. You only spoke that funny English in the old days."

"What do you mean—funny English?" said Fred.

"And what do you mean—old days?" said Sam.

We were about to start another Time Warp Family Brawl, when we reached the ground. No one had time to argue. We had to jump for our lives.

A giant wooden wagon, pulled by two of the biggest horses I have ever seen, came clomping, crashing, rolling toward us. I'm sure you've seen pictures of horses. But let me tell you about horses live and in person. They are way bigger and larger and all-around scarier than book horses.

The wagon driver guy cracked his whip and yelled something at us that I think would get me in a lot of trouble if I wrote it down.

Horses, carts, people, guys pushing carts with rags and boxes and garbage rushed every which way on the stone streets. We were caught in the middle of the 1877 morning rush hour. More drivers yelled more not very pleasant things at us.

"Hey estúpido!" Samza yelled back.

We flattened ourselves against the stone wall of the tower. Freddi pulled Edison back, just before he got squashed by another rumbling wagon.

"Let's get out of here!" I yelled over the noise of wagons and drivers and stones.

"Which way?" yelled Freddi, looking a little rumpled herself.

"Who cares?" said Edison.

We had to get to the library. Our only hope was to find *The Book*, undo whatever time damage we had done, and get Thomas Edison back to normal. I looked around. We were standing in our own city, Brooklyn. More horses clomped past. A nasty smell of garbage, street crud, and horse plop washed over us. I looked around again and realized I had no idea, in my own city, which way to go.

SEVEN

"Joe," said Sam, looking as freaked out as Freddi now. "Your mom works at the library. You go there almost every day to get pizza money from her. Which way is it?"

"That's a hundred years from now," I said. "How should I know?"

"Oh, come on," said Fred. "Brooklyn's not that different. Look. There's the water. Everybody is going that way to get on the ferry to go to work in Manhattan. So this way has to be our neighborhood and Prospect Park and the library. Let's jump."

Fred led the way through a break in traffic. The hundreds of men in old-fashioned suits and ties didn't seem to even see us. They were headed for work . . . and looking pretty strange. Almost every guy had some kind of beard or whiskers and a hat. The few women we saw wore dresses with this poofy part that stuck out like a . . . I don't know exactly what they called it back then. Like a big butt.

"Interesting," said J.

We finally ended up on a quieter side street lined with trees. We were somewhere in Brooklyn Heights. And Fred was right—Brooklyn wasn't that different. The brownstone houses looked just like they do now. There just wasn't a car in sight.

"Wow," said Freddi. "This is so strangela. No flycars or ad-bots or anti-gravity disks. Isn't it romantic?"

"It stinks," said Fred.

He was right. The street water, garbage, and horse smell seemed to be following us.

"No, I mean isn't it amazing that some of this same Brooklyn is still around in your time and our time," said Freddi. "And people are living without all of our modern inventions."

"That definitely stinks," said Fred. "No subway for us to hop on. No phones to order Chinese food. No computers for games."

"No voting for women," said Samza. "No equal rights for everyone."

"They haven't invented Wiffle ball yet," said Fred.

"Now that really stinks," said Samza.

Fred and Samza gave each other a new look, surprised they agreed on something.

"I give up," said Edison, walking in circles around a tree.

"We'd better hurry up and get *The Book*," said Sam, giving Edison a worried look. "And get things fixed up before they get worse . . . like they always do."

"The sooner we get back to our time for Wiffle ball and a slice of pizza, the better," said Fred.

"Get me back to my Synth-Room and Immerseos now," said Samza.

"This way to the Brooklyn Public Library," said Fred.

"No, it's this way," said Sam.

"I think it's this way," I said.

"No, it's not," said J. "We take that street right

over there to Flatbush Avenue. Then we follow Flatbush straight to Prospect Park and the library."

"How do you know that?" said Sam. "Do you have some kind of global mapping invention from your time that always tells you where to go?"

"No," said J. "While you boys were arguing, I asked that nice lady over there for directions to the park."

I know we would have found it anyway, but we followed J's directions over to Flatbush.

It was very weird to see our own city shrunk lower and covered with people who looked like they were from one of those old black-and-white movies. Some of the buildings looked the same— made out of stone and brick stuff. But some were just wooden houses.

The sidewalks were big slabs of stone. The streets were lumpy little stones that bounced and rattled the horse carts rolling over them.

We saw ice wagons, delivery wagons, speedy looking black one-horse carts, and these crazy horsedrawn streetcars that went along railroad tracks right in the street. No gas-powered cars. No electric anything.

I thought the six of us, seven including Edison,

must have looked like we were from Mars, walking down the street in 1877.

That's when I saw the policeman walking right toward us. I had a sinking feeling that looking like we were from Mars might not be a good thing.

J stopped in front of a shop window full of those poofy butt dresses. "Look at the layers on that," she said.

"Impossible," said Samza. "I can't believe they made women wear such things."

The policeman stopped and eyed us. He wore a tall rounded hat and a long blue coat with two rows of gold buttons, and he carried a billy club like you see in those movies where the cops run around and bop each other on the head. Except this guy looked more like a cop who would give you a serious bop and not a funny bop.

J spotted the policeman. "Hola," she said. "I love those buttons. Mucho bonito. And the hat. The hat is just—"

"Come on, you weenie," said Edison.

"He said he has a beanie," said Freddi, pulling Edison along.

The policeman gave us a funny look like he was going to start asking us questions.

"Visitors from Mexico," I explained, pushing everyone along. "And China. Lots of things different there. Going to library now. Bye!"

"Adios."

"Zai jian."

The policeman watched our strange group make its way down Flatbush Avenue. The last I saw of him, he was still scratching the back of his head with his billy club. I think he just couldn't decide what to ask us first.

As we walked along Flatbush Avenue, farther out into Brooklyn, it was amazing to see everything change around us. I knew things would look different, but I didn't think they would look this different.

The streets became dirt and mud instead of stone. There were big empty spaces and fields between buildings. We almost lost Freddi, she was so excited to see real sheep and cows. I think I recognized some of the churches from our time. Though in this time of 1877, they were the biggest things around.

"I can't believe it," said J. "How do you live in such an old-fashioned time?"

Fred looked at her like she was nuts. "We don't live like this," he said. "We have cars and jets and phones."

"It's the same thing," said J. "How do you live without teleports and microbots?"

I was about to ask J exactly what these new things were that people in the future couldn't live without. That's when I saw Seventh Avenue and had a terrible thought. Seventh Avenue in our time is a very busy street covered with stores and churches and buildings. This Seventh Avenue looked deserted—half built, half empty fields.

"Uh guys . . . I think we'd better hurry and get to the library."

We walked down the wide, kind-of spooky, empty streets and made it to the big traffic circle where the library, the arch, and the entrance to the park are.

"Whoa," said Fred.

"Uh-oh," said Sam.

"So what," said Edison.

Of course there were no cars in the big, wide-open circle. I expected that.

But there was no arch, and no fancy columns at the entrance to the park. I hadn't expected that.

And most unexpected of all—there was no Brooklyn Public Library.

EIGHT

We all stood staring at the spot where we thought we would see the Brooklyn Public Library. We all stood staring at the spot where we thought we were going to find *The Book*. We all stood staring at nothing but a bunch of bushes.

Sam squeezed his forehead with one hand. "You have got to be kidding. Wait. Don't tell me. Let me guess. The library isn't built yet."

Samza touched the side of her glasses. "They won't even start building it here until 1912."

"I told you not to tell me," said Sam. "And how do you know? And why didn't you tell us before we came all the way out here?"

Samza held out her black glasses. "My invention—my Memory Specs—tells me everything I need to know. And nobody asked me before."

"Those aren't glasses?" said Fred.

"Nobody needs glasses in the twenty-first

century," said Samza. "These are a fashion statement."

"Right," said Fred.

"I give up," said Edison. He sat down on a bench.

"I'm with you," said Sam, sitting next to him.

J looked all around the big wide-open circle. I'm sure it looked completely different from how it looked in her time, too. She flipped her hair back and gave Sam and Edison a determined look.

"We can't give up," said J. "If we don't find *The Book* and get history back on track in this time, there's no telling what will happen in the future."

"It might be more peaceful," said Freddi. "Look at those horse carriages. There are real live sheep in the park."

49

"There might be no electricity, no movies, no Brooklyn Bridge," said Samza.

Fred made a face. "And look at that steaming pile of horse—"

"So what," said Edison.

Sam kicked a small rock. "Well, ask genius girl and her brain glasses where we should look for *The Book*."

Samza kicked the same rock back. "Tell genius boy my invention is a database of information . . . not a fortune teller."

"We are so dead," said Sam. "Trapped in the old-fashioned past . . . with the most annoying people from the future."

"It's your own fault," said Samza.

"Be quiet," said Sam.

"Make me."

"I don't make monkeys, I just train them. . . ."

"Ahhhhhhh!" yelled Fred, pulling on his Cyclones hat. "You guys are driving me nuts. Joe—do something before we all go crazy. Don't you know a *Book*-finder trick? Or at least a food-finder trick? We're going to die of starvation before anything else."

"Oh sure," I said. "Here. I'll use my magic rope

to make a whole magic picnic and—" I jammed my hand into my pocket. My rope was gone. I checked my other pocket. Empty.

Everything was going wrong.

That's when I saw the end of my rope sticking out from under one of the bushes that would become the Brooklyn Public Library in about thirty years.

I picked up the end of the rope.

Something pulled back.

I pulled harder.

And out of the bushes, tied to the other end of the rope, came a small blue book with strange silver designs and writing.

It was *The Book*.

"Nice trick," said Fred.

NINE

I held *The Book* in my hands. I couldn't believe it. My trick rope had actually worked . . . sort of.

"See you some other time, girls," said Fred.

"And get to work on those inventions," said Sam to Thomas Alva Edison.

I untied the rope and opened *The Book*. We all braced ourselves for that strange roller-coaster, inside-out, wake-up-in-the-middle-of-a-dream, time-travel feeling, and . . . and . . . and nothing happened.

I closed *The Book* and flipped it open again. Nothing.

Fred, Sam, J, Freddi, and Samza looked at me.

I checked the page. There was an old photo of the Brooklyn Bridge with just the towers up. Right where we started. It had to be the right page.

I closed *The Book*. I opened it.

No green mist. No time warping. No nothing.

"Come on Joe," said Sam, sounding a little nervous. "Quit fooling around."

"Okay," I said. I closed *The Book*. I gently rubbed its cover. I had no idea what I was doing. I opened to the picture of the Brooklyn Bridge and—

"Come on, you weenie," said Edison.

Sam looked completely terrified. And I wasn't feeling too good myself. Our neighborhood in 1877 was interesting, but not interesting enough for us to spend the rest of our lives there, with our great-granddaughters, and a messed-up Thomas Edison.

"Let me see," said J.

I realized it was her *Book* too, one hundred years after I had it—have it, whatever. "Good idea, I said. "Maybe you can start it."

J closed *The Book* then opened it.

Still nothing.

"I think you guys wrecked it," said J. "Samza?"

Samza pushed her Memory Specs up on top of her head and took *The Book*. She flipped back and forth, scanning pages and checking things. "Ha hmmm. Ummm. I see." She touched her Memory Specs and flipped some more pages. She closed *The Book* and looked up.

We all leaned forward, staring at her.

"Well?" said Sam.

"Nah, it's fine," said Samza. "Just as I thought. You need to either deactivate the Sonic Warp or reset the Spatial Coordinates."

"Say what?" said Fred.

"Say the voice command you used to warp us here," said Freddi, translating into plain English. "Or we have to take *The Book* back to the exact spot where we first appeared in this time."

Sam shook his head. "No way. There is no way I am climbing back up that suicide tower to meet up with that mutant space alien again."

"Well, just say the stupid voice command you recorded to get us here," said Samza.

Sam grabbed his head with both hands (like he does when he's really annoyed with us). "I keep telling you—I didn't give it any commands. I was minding my own business, working on wiring my digital Graphi-Sonic when Joe pulled out *The Book* and—"

"So what," said Edison.

Sam looked at Edison. And if lightbulbs had been invented, one would have lit up over his head. "And that's it! I was talking about Edison just before we warped. And all this time he's been saying exactly what we said. One of those must be the voice command."

We all got the same idea at the same time. We all started talking at *The Book*.

"I give up."

"Come on, you weenie."

"So what."

We stood back, ready to time warp out of there.

Nothing happened. Not even a puff of pale green time traveling mist.

Samza closed *The Book* and tucked it under her arm. "Looks like it's back to the top of the Brooklyn Bridge."

"Wait," said Sam, turning pale green himself. He bent down and spoke to *The Book*. "Abracadabra. Help, save me. I am Sam. Sam I am."

Freddi, not looking too good herself, joined Sam. "Testing, testing. Onetwothreefour. Unodostres."

Nothing.

Sam and Freddi looked at each other, then both yelled into *The Book,* "HELLLLLLLLLLLLLLP!"

TEN

"I think we have to go back to the bridge," said J.

Sam and Freddi looked sick.

"I'm too young to die one hundred years before I'm born," said Sam.

"Me too," said Freddi. "Two hundred years before I'm born."

"Isn't there some other way?" I said. "If *The Book* recorded the voice command, it must be able to play it back."

Samza thought about that for a minute. "Maybe."

"Or what if we take *The Book* to the exact spot where my house is going to be?" I said. "That's exactly where we warped from."

Samza thought about that for a minute. "Maybe."

"I give up," said Edison.

"Well, let's do something before I strangle this

guy," said Fred. "He's really starting to bug me."

I didn't think the world would appreciate Fred strangling the inventor of the phonograph and the lightbulb before he invented them. So I led everyone into the park, and headed for my house . . . or at least to where my house would be in another year or two, or ten or twenty.

I knew where we were going because, like Sam said, I walk it almost every day. It's a straight shot from my house to the library.

So this walk was exactly the same, but completely different. We were all in exactly the same neighborhood we lived in, but we were in a completely different time. We were walking from the library to my house, but there was no library, and no my house.

Time Warping is funny like that.

We walked into the park and the weird feeling got weirder. The park looked mostly the same, just newer.

"Prospect Park. Five hundred and twenty-six acres, opened in 1866," said Samza, checking with her Specs.

In our time, we were used to seeing kids throwing Frisbees, flying kites, walking around,

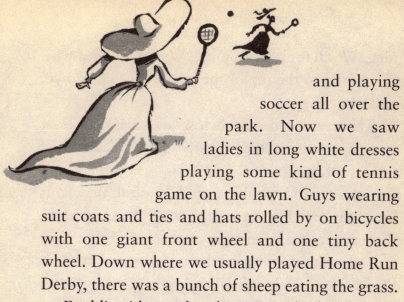

and playing soccer all over the park. Now we saw ladies in long white dresses playing some kind of tennis game on the lawn. Guys wearing suit coats and ties and hats rolled by on bicycles with one giant front wheel and one tiny back wheel. Down where we usually played Home Run Derby, there was a bunch of sheep eating the grass.

Freddi said exactly what I was thinking. "This is so time warpy. It's exactly like when we live here. But it's not."

We walked along the path, trying not to attract too much attention. We had almost made it out of the park when Fred stopped short.

"Wait. What's that?"

We all looked around. Was it the kids in funny shorts and socks? The ladies with the sun umbrellas? The evil-looking guy with the big curling moustache? Police?

Fred took off running. We all took off running. We had no idea why. We ran up to the top of the hill. We looked down, and saw why.

There, spread out below us, were at least twenty wooden tables covered with chicken, and roast beef, and salad, and corn, and apples, and lemonade, and cookies, and . . . and use your imagination. Fill in just about every mouth-watering food a hungry person could imagine. Kids ran all around. Guys in short gray pants to their knees ate and laughed and joked. They were wearing what maybe looked like baseball hats.

Down in the field, people were standing in a familiar diamond pattern. They were playing what definitely looked like baseball!

Fred closed his eyes and took a giant sniff. "Mmmmmm. Food. Baseball. This old-time Brooklyn may be okay after all. Come on," he said, heading for the food.

"But how—" I started to say.

Fred pointed to the big white banner over the main table.

In big block letters it said, WELCOME BROOKLYN BASE-BALL PLAYERS.

Fred tipped his Cyclones baseball cap. He

pointed to Freddi's cap. "We're from Brooklyn. We are Base-ball Players."

We knew we had to get *The Book* working and save the history of the world. But we also knew we were too hungry to think about that.

We followed Fred down into the picnic, and tore into the food. We all loaded up plates with everything in sight, and joined in the crowd as best we could, while eating as much as possible.

"From Mexico, sí," said J with a mouthful of chicken.

"Clothes are very different in China," I said to the lady with the cookies.

"Yeah, we're sorta from around here," said Fred.

"Mmmmm," said Thomas Edison, eating nothing but cookies.

"You've seen the great bridge?" asked a little girl in pigtails and a dress.

"Seen it?" said Sam, washing down a second sandwich with a paper cone cup of lemonade. "We've been on the very top of the tower," bragged Sam.

"Glued to the handrail." Samza laughed.

The warming sun drifted in and out of a few perfectly white clouds in the blue sky. We sat on the grass and started watching the baseball game.

We were full. We had *The Book*. With a few minor adjustments, we were almost home. I remember thinking, "This is almost too good to be true." So of course it was—too good to be true.

"You two!" called a baseball player from the third base line.

We all looked behind us.

"You two." The guy pointed at Fred and Freddi. "Get over here. We need you in the game right now."

"We're not really—" began Freddi.

"—not really infielders. We'll play outfield," said Fred, pulling Freddi to her feet. "Come on. We'll show these old-fashioned types how to play some modern baseball. How tough can they be? Look at these guys. They pitch underhand."

Fred dragged Freddi into the outfield—Fred in center, Freddi in right. We moved over to watch.

The inning started. We cheered. It was sort of baseball like we know it. There were three bases, home plate, a bat, and a ball. But only the pitcher and the catcher wore gloves. And the pitcher was just kind of lobbing them over with an underhand toss. There didn't seem to be any balls or strikes. Definitely a hitter's game.

After four or five hits in a row, the next batter grounded one to the shortstop. He scooped up the ball. But then he pegged it right at the guy running for third, and hit him in the back.

"Out!" yelled someone.

"What the heck was that?" I said. "He didn't tag him. He hit him with the ball."

A lady in a big saucer-shaped hat in front of me turned around. "It's those Massachusetts rules. New York rules say tag the runner. Much better."

"No kidding," said Sam. "Especially for the runner. So how come they're playing Massachusetts rules in Brooklyn?"

The lady pointed to the next batter. "Mug says he likes it better that way."

"Mug?" said Sam.

We looked at the next batter's meaty hands, hairy face, and general mutant killer look.

"Like Ugly Mug, the Mutant-Space-Alien-Guard-Brooklyn-Bridge-Fred-Beaned-with-the-Rock-and-Who-Probably-Still-Wants-to-Club-Us Mug?" said Sam.

"Exactamente," I said.

"Yikes."

"Exactamente."

ELEVEN

The pitcher lobbed his first pitch.

Ugly Mug swung and ripped a line drive that knocked off the pitcher's glove, his hat, and almost his head.

Then things got like our new friend's name—ugly.

Ugly Mug's team scored six straight runs. There was no way this pitcher was going to get anybody out. Fred must have thought the same thing.

"Time out," he called and jogged in to the mound.

Ugly Mug squinted at Fred. "Hey, it's you!"

Fred got the ball from the pitcher. He roughed it up on one side. Then he showed the pitcher how to snap it throwing overhand.

"He's showing him how to throw an overhand curve ball," said Sam. "Now Ugly Mug is really going to kill us."

Fred went back to center field. The pitcher threw his new overhand curve. And the next three guys topped three weak little grounders for outs.

The crowd buzzed. Ugly Mug stared at Fred.

Then things got really ugly.

Guess who took over as the next pitcher. How did you know? Ugly Mug. He pounded the ball into his mitt.

"Sam," I said. "I have a feeling we're not going to make it back to my house or the Brooklyn Bridge. Try some more voice commands. Quick!"

Samza flipped open *The Book* for Sam. "You can do it."

"Come on, you weenie," said Edison.

"Zip it," said Samza. "That's my great-grand-father you're talking to, and he grows up to be just as famous an inventor as . . . well just never mind. Go Sam."

Sam was stunned, and interested, and proud of Samza all at once.

Ugly Mug wound up and blazed a fastball right over the top of Fred's head. He looked like he had already practiced plenty of overhand throwing himself.

Sam got to work, speaking into *The Book*.

"Graphi-Sonic . . . Voice-a-tronic . . . Wiffle-Matic?"

Nothing.

Fred dug in at the plate. Ugly Mug fired another fastball. He wasn't even trying to throw strikes.

Fred fell back in the dirt.

"Eenie, meanie, mynie, mo!" said Sam. "Here we go! I don't know!"

Nothing from *The Book*.

Samza adjusted her glasses and looked closely at *The Book*. "Joe, I think you might be right."

Fred dusted himself off and dug his back foot in at the plate. Now he was mad.

"Right about what?" I said, watching Ugly Mug squint his already beady eyes at Fred.

"I think *The Book* can play back the voice command," said Samza. "And this green stripe right here is a groove just like Edison used in his first Talking Machine. We just need a needle to play it."

"Yes!" said Sam.

But we were too late.

Ugly Mug had already uncorked his own revenge beanball pitch at Fred. "Oh no," said the lady in the huge white hat in front of me. Even she knew what was going to happen. But what Ugly Mug and the lady didn't know about Fred is that Fred is a real player. He doesn't just outplay you. He outthinks you. I've lost enough Wiffle-ball games to know.

Fred knew exactly what kind of pitch was coming. He had already stepped back. He set himself, swung, and spanked the ball to right center. By the time the center fielder got the ball back in, Fred was standing on second base.

"Boo-yah!" I yelled, imitating Fred's favorite SportsCenter announcer. Ugly Mug did not look happy.

This was just too good . . . until we saw the next batter who had to face him—Freddi.

"Guys, find us a needle," I said. "Sam, play *The Book* now."

Sam and J were way ahead of me. J pulled a long straight pin from the lady's hat in front of us. Sam was messing around with his empty paper cup.

"I did this once
with a record and an
old record player," said Sam.
"You need the paper cone to amplify the sound
waves. Otherwise you'll never hear it."

Samza and Edison looked on, amazed.

Ugly Mug pounded the ball into his glove.
Freddi took a half a practice swing and stepped up
to the plate. I didn't know which was going to be
worse—Ugly Mug beaning Freddi, or Fred charg-
ing the mound to attack Ugly Mug for beaning
Freddi.

Sam pushed the pin through the small end

of the paper cone and dragged it across the groove in *The Book*. I heard a tiny voice come out of the paper cone. So did Sam. So did Samza. So did a completely amazed Thomas Alva Edison.

Ugly Mug rocked back on one leg.

"That's it!" said Sam. He dragged the needle over the groove once more to be sure.

Ugly Mug fired the ball right at Freddi with everything he had.

"Mary had a little lamb!" shouted Sam.

The Book beeped and flashed a voice print pattern. Something popped. The whole baseball diamond suddenly tinted time-traveling mist green. Weirder still—everything clicked into slow motion.

The beanball pitch floated slowly toward home. Edison caught Sam's pin/paper cone invention and stared at it. You could almost see a lightbulb go on over his head. Freddi had all day to smile, step back, and time one big sweet swing at the ball like it was set up on a tee.

The instant she connected, something popped again. Time warped back to real time. The ball rocketed over the left fielder's head. A healthy green mist cycloned over our 1877 Prospect Park baseball game in fast forward time.

"Boo-yah!" cheered the lady in the white hat.

Without a second to say good-bye, adios, or zai jian to our great-granddaughters; without knowing what would happen to Thomas Edison and his inventions, Washington Roebling and his Brooklyn Bridge, or Ugly Mug and his baseball career; like Freddi's home run crush, we were going going boo-yah gone.

Inventors' Corner

Thomas Edison didn't remember anything about his adventure with the Time Warp Trio. He went on to invent a machine that could replay sound, a dependable electric lightbulb, and about 1,091 other things.

Washington and Emily Roebling saw the Brooklyn Bridge project to completion on May 24, 1883. They never told anyone about visitors from Mexico and China studying knots on the bridge.

Fred, inspired by Ugly Mug and the Massachusetts Base-Ball rules, invented his own Wiffle Bean-ball Game. You get points for home runs and for beaning your opponent.

Joe invented his own rope trick, but won't show anybody how it's done.

Sam is still working on his Graphi-Sonic. Right now, it looks like this:

But whatever he invents, he swears he will never, never let it get anywhere near a certain thin, blue, covered-with-silver-designs . . . *Book*.

You can make your own invention. Use 1 percent inspiration and 99 percent perspiration. Think up something. Then get sweaty and make it.